If you're happy and you know it

Penny Dann

little ORCHARD

If you're happy and you know it,
clap your hands;
If you're happy and you know it,
clap your hands;

this

little ORCHARD

book belongs to

....

....

SOUTHWARK LIBRARIES

SK 0654278 6

For Ellie and Luca

ORCHARD BOOKS
338 Euston Road, London NW1 3BH
Orchard Books Australia
Level 17/207 Kent Street, Sydney, NSW 2000
First published in 2001 by Orchard Books
This edition published in 2003
978 1 84362 219 2
Illustrations © Penny Dann 2001
The right of Penny Dann to be identified as
the illustrator of this work has been asserted by her
in accordance with the Copyright, Design and Patents Act, 1988.
A CIP catalogue record for this book is available from the British Library.
1 3 5 7 9 10 8 6 4 2
Printed in China
Orchard Books is a division of Hachette Children's Books,
an Hachette Livre UK company.

If you're happy and you know it
And you really want to show it,

If you're happy and you know it,
clap your hands.

If you're happy
and you know it,
stamp your feet;

If you're happy
and you know it,
stamp your feet;

If you're happy and you know it
And you really want to show it,

If you're happy and you know it,
stamp your feet.

If you're happy and you know it,
wave your hand;
If you're happy and you know it,
wave your hand;

If you're happy and you know it
And you really want to show it,

If you're happy and you know it,
wave your hand.

If you're happy
and you know it,
nod your head;

If you're happy
and you know it,
nod your head;

If you're happy and you know it
And you really want to show it,

If you're happy and you know it,
nod your head.

If you're happy and you know it,
touch your toes;
If you're happy and you know it,
touch your toes;

If you're happy and you know it
And you really want to show it,

If you're happy and you know it,
touch your toes.

If you're happy
and you know it,
swing your arms;

If you're happy
and you know it,
swing your arms;

If you're happy and you know it
And you really want to show it,

If you're happy and you know it,
swing your arms.

If you're happy
and you know it,
hop around;

If you're happy
and you know it,
hop around;

If you're happy and you know it
And you really want to show it,

If you're happy and you know it,
hop around.

If you're happy and you know it,
shout, "We are!"
If you're happy and you know it,
shout, "We are!"

We are!

If you're happy and you know it
And you really want to show it,
If you're happy and you know it,
shout, "We are!"

We are !